I GET SO HUNGRY

I GET SO Hungry

Bebe Moore Campbell

Illustrated by Amy Bates

G. P. PUTNAM'S SONS

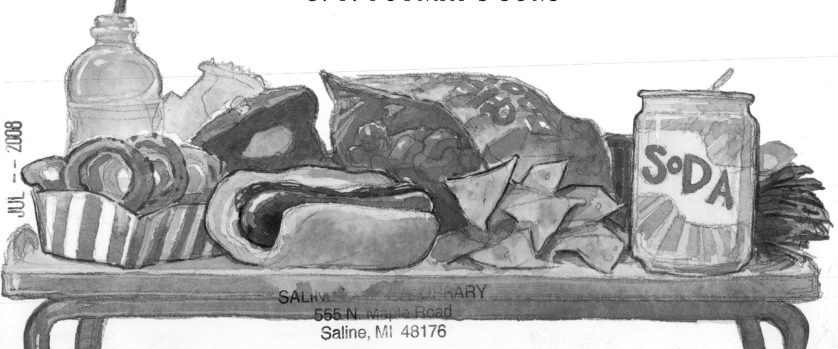

On the first day of school

I walk into my new classroom and standing in the middle is a rainbow woman.

"Good morning," she says as kids stream into the room. "My name is Mrs. Theodora Patterson. I'm your new teacher."

She pulls a hat from the box by her desk and places it on her head. "The first day of school is Thinking Cap Day," she says with a wink, then laughs.

My friends Keisha, Sarah, and I laugh too.

While Mrs. Patterson is taking attendance, Sarah asks Keisha, "What did you do this summer?"

"Went to visit my grandma in Atlanta," Keisha says.

"Went to visit my grandma in Atlanta," someone repeats in a pretend baby voice. It is Arnold Inksley. We roll our eyes.

"I went to camp," Sarah says. "I hiked."

They look at me. "I stayed home and — " I say.

" — ate everything in the house," Arnold says. "Hey, Supersize, don't break the desk."

"Not funny," Sarah tells Arnold.

Potato chips always make me feel better when I'm sad. No one is supposed to eat in class, but I can't resist. When Mrs. Patterson isn't looking, I slip my hand inside my lunch box and sneak a few chips.

I'm still a little sad at lunchtime. I swallow my mom's fried chicken, two biscuits, a thick piece of cake and a soda so fast, I can barely taste them. I gobble down half of Keisha's sandwich and Sarah's banana too. Once I start eating, it's hard to stop.

After a while, Mrs. Patterson takes off her hat and blows a whistle. "It's read-to-a-friend time," she announces.

"Come on," Sarah says, and I follow her to the book basket. "Once upon a time, there was a beautiful princess," she reads.

Princesses are always skinny.

During reading time, I hear crunching. Mrs. Patterson pretends that she is looking in her purse for something. Then she coughs, and I see her shove a cookie in her mouth.

I can hear Mrs. Patterson breathing when she gets up and walks to the blackboard. She starts writing numbers.

When Mrs. Patterson has finished, she takes a big floppy hat from her box and places it on her head. All the kids laugh. "Is there a problem?" she asks.

"Yes, there is a problem," the class says. "A math problem!"

A few of us raise our hands and a tall boy in the back says, "Oooh, I know, I know!"

Mrs. Patterson calls on me. "What's the answer, Nikki?"

"Fourteen," I say with a great big smile.

Mrs. Patterson smiles back at me. "Good for you," she says.

"Nikki Thicky is Fatty Patty's pet," Arnold whispers.

"Be quiet, Arnold," Keisha says as other kids laugh.

I want to say something mean, but I just sneak more potato chips. I pretend that each chip is Arnold Inksley and I eat until he is gone.

Keisha, Sarah and I sit together on the way home. We sing radio songs. I sing the lead, and they do the backup. Everybody on the bus claps at the end. When we grow up, we're going to start a real singing group: Nikki and the Harmonies.

"Bye, Nikki Thicky," Arnold calls out as the bus stops.

Mom and I have fried fish, french fries and soda for dinner. Every time I think about Arnold and skinny princesses, I eat some more.

In October, Mom and I visit Dr. Chavez for checkups. After he weighs us, he shakes his head. "No more junk food," he says.

"Absolutely," Mom says. She smiles at Dr. Chavez and nods.

When we reach our block, I can hear the doughnuts calling. *Nikki, come taste me. Nikki, please eat me.*

"Let's have a doughnut," Mom says. "It's been a long morning. We deserve a little treat."

On Monday, when I go to my classroom, there's a stranger at Mrs. Patterson's desk. Later, I hear the other teachers whispering in the hall. One says, "Close call." Another says, "Too heavy."

When I get home, I ask my mom, "Can we go on a diet?"

"A diet?" Mom laughs. "We come from a long line of big-boned women. We'll never be Skinny Minnies."

But I don't want to be so big anymore.

"Fatty Patty's back," whispers Arnold when we return to school after Christmas.

Mrs. Patterson is back, too, but something is different about her. Her pants and top seem too large, and she is wearing sneakers. All day she sips from a bottle of water. She doesn't crunch once.

The next morning, when Keisha, Sarah and I arrive at school, we see Mrs. Patterson walking around the school yard very slowly. Mrs. Patterson now walks every day. "My New Year's resolution is to eat less and exercise more," she tells me. I hope she doesn't turn into a Skinny Minny.

In class she puts on her silly bookworm hat, but I don't laugh. I feel hungry and lonesome.

At home, I tell my mom what Mrs. Patterson is doing. I reach out for chips, then stop. "If Mrs. Patterson says it's okay, may I walk with her before school? I'll take the early bus."

Mom gives me a funny look. "Okay," she says.

Every morning Mrs. Patterson and I walk.

"What do you do when you get hungry?"
I ask her one day.

"I don't get as hungry because I eat lots of
good food."

"You eat a lot? But you're getting thinner."

"Yes, because I eat the right things," she says.
"No sodas, no fried food, and fruits and vegetables
instead of cakes and doughnuts."

"What about potato chips?" I ask.

"A few. But only once in a while. What's the
matter, Nikki?"

I start to cry. "My mom won't buy me the food you eat."

"Well, what if you try to eat a little less and move a lot more? And only eat when you're hungry, not when you're sad or angry or bored? If you fill your life with interesting things to do, you won't feel so hungry all the time. What do you like to do?"

"Sing," I say.

"Let me hear you."

I sing a few notes.

"That's beautiful!"

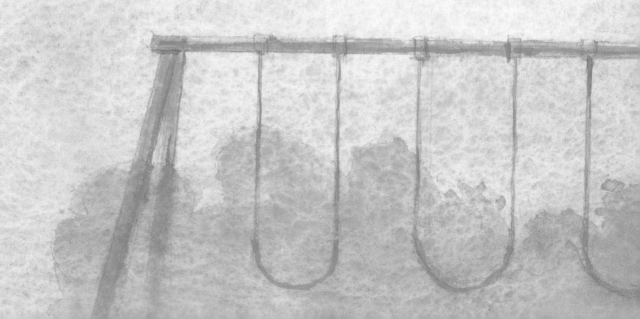

In the spring, Mom comes for teacher conference. At the end, I hear her say, "Mrs. Patterson, how did you lose all that weight since I last saw you?"

"I've cut junk food out of my diet and I'm walking every day. Nikki has been a great morning walking partner," Mrs. Patterson says.

"Maybe I'll be your weekend partner," Mom says to me.

The first Saturday, I have to pull Mom out of bed. We walk around the block once, very slowly. But by the end of the first month, she can go around five times.

That Monday, I can't wait to tell Mrs. Patterson.

"Nikki Thicky," Arnold Inksley yells as my teacher and I are smiling together.

"Hey, Arnold, open your eyes. The only thing fat around here is your mouth!" Keisha and Sarah say. Even Arnold Inksley laughs. The sound fills me up better than potato chips.

This book is dedicated to those individuals and organizations
who are working to challenge the forces and factors that
contribute to childhood obesity.

This book is also dedicated to the loving memory of Bebe Moore Campbell, an
indomitable spirit who left us much too soon, and the wonderful angels who
supported Bebe as well as her family during her illness.

•

G. P. PUTNAM'S SONS
A division of Penguin Young Readers Group.
Published by The Penguin Group.
Penguin Group (USA) Inc., 375 Hudson Street, New York, NY 10014, U.S.A.
Penguin Group (Canada), 90 Eglinton Avenue East, Suite 700, Toronto, Ontario M4P 2Y3, Canada (a division of Pearson Penguin
Canada Inc.). Penguin Books Ltd, 80 Strand, London WC2R 0RL, England. Penguin Ireland, 25 St. Stephen's Green, Dublin 2, Ireland
(a division of Penguin Books Ltd.). Penguin Group (Australia), 250 Camberwell Road, Camberwell, Victoria 3124, Australia (a division
of Pearson Australia Group Pty Ltd). Penguin Books India Pvt Ltd, 11 Community Centre, Panchsheel Park, New Delhi - 110 017,
India. Penguin Group (NZ), 67 Apollo Drive, Rosedale, North Shore 0632, New Zealand (a division of Pearson New Zealand Ltd).
Penguin Books (South Africa) (Pty) Ltd, 24 Sturdee Avenue, Rosebank, Johannesburg 2196, South Africa. Penguin Books Ltd, Registered
Offices: 80 Strand, London WC2R 0RL, England.

Text copyright © 2008 by Bebe Moore Campbell.
Illustrations copyright © 2008 by Amy Bates.

Manufactured in China by South China Printing Co. Ltd. Design by Richard Amari. Text set in 14.5 pt Book Antiqua Bold.

Library of Congress Cataloging-in-Publication Data
Campbell, Bebe Moore, 1950–2006.
I get so hungry / by Bebe Moore Campbell ; illustrated by Amy Bates. p. cm.
Summary: When her teacher suffers health problems because of her weight,
Nikki, who is always getting teased about her size, decides she wants to live
a healthier lifestyle. [1. Schools—Fiction. 2. Teachers—Fiction. 3. Weight
control—Fiction.] I. Bates, Amy June, ill. II. Title.
PZ7.C15079Ig 2008   [E]—dc22   2007014117

ISBN 978-0-399-24311-0
1 3 5 7 9 10 8 6 4 2